PLOVER NIVOLA SERIES

ON THE WINDOW LICKS THE NIGHT

John Mitchell's first collection, *Alaska Stories*, won a Pushcart Prize in 1984. He has subsequently co-translated four Latin-American novels into English, three by Mexicans and one by a Cuban. He summers in Alaska and winters in Hawaii.

ALSO BY JOHN MITCHELL

Fiction

Alaska Stories
Exile in Alaska

Translation

Notes of a Villager by José Rubén Romero
Calling All Heroes by Paco Ignacio Taibo II
Qwert and the Wedding Gown by Matías Montes Huidobro
Gray Skies Tomorrow by Silvia Molina

ON THE WINDOW LICKS THE NIGHT

A Nivola
by
John Mitchell

Plover Press • Kaneohe, Hawaii • 1994

Copyright © 1994 John Mitchell
All rights reserved. For information, address the publisher,
Plover Press, P.O. Box R, Kaneohe, Hawaii 96744.

Printed and bound in the United States of America.

Cover Illustration by Ming Li Jiang

Library of Congress Cataloging-in-Publication Data

Mitchell, John, 1930–
On the window licks the night : a nivola / by John Mitchell.
  p.   cm. — (Plover nivola series)
ISBN 0-917635-18-3 (pbk.) : $8.95
1. Creative writing—Study and teaching—California—Fiction.
2. Psychiatric hospital patients—California—Fiction. 3. Authors,
American—California—Fiction. I. Title. II. Series.
PS3563.I767405   1994
813'.54—dc20   93-48949
                                                              CIP

Distributed by The Talman Company, Inc.
131 Spring St., New York, NY 10012

To Margo

The host, he says that all is well
And the fire-wood glow is bright;
The food has a warm and tempting smell,—
But on the window licks the night.

Pile on the logs. . . . Give me your hands,
Friends! No,—it is not fright. . . .
But hold me . . . somewhere I heard demands. . . .
And on the window licks the night.
—HART CRANE

And I, to alter pernicious custom, changing
the terms . . . novel to *nivola*.
—MIGUEL DE UNAMUNO

1

I make a blue car pass through the gates. On its bumper is a rental sticker of the kind that instantly marks the driver as an outsider. I'm satisfied with the car, but not with the visitor. I want him to show a little more uncertainty, to be torn between curiosity and dread, as most travelers to this "campus" are. Three doors from the office of the patients' rights advocate he succumbs to the blandishments of a little man waving a baseball cap and pulls over. Immediately his car is surrounded, giving it the look of a large roll covered with flies. From my bedroom window I can't hear the words, but the sign language is one of increasing frustration. Finally the visitor pulls away, aided like a horse by slaps from the baseball cap. He is clearly looking for a way out of here. Then he sees me waving as I come out of the dormitory, and his teeth reveal themselves in

John Mitchell

an embarrassed grin. He pulls to a stop and jumps out.

"Lucky I don't take no for an answer," he says. "The people on the corner told me you had just left for Alaska."

I glance down the street and have to thank these ever-watchful "clients" for their infinite willingness to believe each other's stories. As a hideout, Camarillo is the perfect place, and the weather is so much better than Alaska's.

"Come on in," I say, "I've been waiting for you."

"Are you sure you're the famous writer?"

I smile noncommittally. What does he want me to do, reveal the ending? Later, when the interview is well under way, I might let him in on the time I killed my parents, but that's a long way down the trail. For the present, my concern is to get him past the wonders of the wing in which lobotomies were once performed and away from the dining room where today metal knives and forks are permitted, but with the result the mess hall sounds even more like the Tower of Babel. Seven years ago my father

On the Window Licks the Night

said I was being led down a street by pied pipers, and now I want to tell my story.

Camarillo, California. The author's face is backlit by the window, adding darkness to his already sunburned skin. His eyes are ultramarine, the sort a primitive might call evil and whose intensity would disconcert some people. In a different setting his lack of flesh would suggest conditioning, but here the muscle definition is the result of a Spartan diet. He is sitting in a rocker which he chose as you would an athlete, on the fourth or fifth round, when he and his sister dismantled their parents' house. Next to it is a footstool covered with needlepoint which his mother completed from a preprinted design during those long evenings when she was recovering from one of a series of abdominal operations which were socially fashionable at the time. Since the furniture of childhood was shipped, everything has gone downhill. In the dry desert air wood develops cracks, and before the interview begins the author wonders aloud if these are really the same pieces he used to

John Mitchell

stand in awe of as a boy. Although the bedsheets are neatly tucked with hospital corners, the arrangement of objects around him suggests the same air of informality I saw in the street. He is wearing only bathing trunks. A neat pile of fingernails on the window sill testifies to the good condition of his teeth. Far off across the Simi Valley an old church bell is ringing.

INTERVIEWER: I'm glad you finally agreed to this meeting.
AUTHOR: We both know I've done nothing but dream about it all my life. It was nice of you to come.
INTERVIEWER: We always try to cooperate with the state. Besides, the atmosphere is totally different from the public's image of a mental institution. It's more like a Boy Scout camp.
AUTHOR: I sometimes think so myself (laughs).
INTERVIEWER: All right, let's get down to business. I want you to tell me about yourself. How was it you got into writing?
AUTHOR: That's a little hard to say. I was imaginative, but so are many children, more so than I

was. In the beginning writing was just an avocation. I was even out for football.

INTERVIEWER: Would it be fair to say you were having mental problems then?

AUTHOR: They were the result, not the cause. I was like a fox growing up in a family of chickens, thinking he's a rooster. Then one day he happens to eat one and realizes he is somehow different. I must have been, for I'm here, you're there.

INTERVIEWER: How did your family like the idea of your writing?

AUTHOR: Their near panic was almost laughable. At the time, they were pushing me hard to go to college, and when I wouldn't agree my mother began quoting Governor Bradford of the Plymouth Colony, who warned gold seekers that only those who worked would be fed. "Those which works, ets; them that don't starve." My father, who went in somewhat less for verbal games, was first amused, then concerned, and finally so upset he sent me to a psychiatrist.

INTERVIEWER: What was the doctor's diagnosis?

John Mitchell

AUTHOR: I refused to answer his questions.

INTERVIEWER: You didn't think he could help?

AUTHOR: He was just a patsy. My sister and I never had intimate conversations with my parents. Whenever we had problems, a paid professional was called in whose job it was to satisfy their wishes.

INTERVIEWER: And yet you seem to love their furniture.

AUTHOR: Their disapproval had nothing to do with me. Each was responding to perceived failings on the part of his or her own parents, which of course was only a reaction to the generation before. Since my maternal grandfather had been a speculator, my mother was determined that I should have a so-called respectable profession. She never talked of her father except as a man who had willfully sacrificed her security to playing the market. Following the Crash of '28, she had to sew every stitch of clothing she wore on her back and she never forgave him. Whenever I mentioned his name, she would go into a paroxysm of slavering and rub her hands together like Shylock, saying "Schemes! Schemes! Schemes!" In college she'd majored in drama, and

On the Window Licks the Night

sometimes it was very hard to tell when she was acting. In addition to talking like an illiterate and imitating Shylock, she would sometimes weep and wail, and the only clue to her true feelings was my father's laughter, and sometimes not even that. Once I caught her alone in her room, pitifully knocking her wrists together as if waiting to be handcuffed. I laughed uproariously, but her words stopped me cold. "You're just like your father." "You mean you were really crying?" "Of course, I was." With her it was often very hard to tell.

INTERVIEWER: If your mother's conditioning inclined her toward the straight and narrow, what about your father's?

AUTHOR: Enemas.

INTERVIEWER: Enemas? I think you'll have to be a little more specific.

AUTHOR: Before his mother passed away, diabetes had so weakened her she was unable to move her bowels naturally. The disability resulted in a rather unpleasant procedure on which I stumbled once or twice. It also turned me into a regularity freak, so much so I used to beg for suppositories.

John Mitchell

INTERVIEWER: And did they always give you suppositories?

AUTHOR: Only when they felt I'd really earned one. Fifteen years later when I asked my father to underwrite a year in Rome or Paris so I could write, all he had to do was mention her name and we both understood it was impossible and why.

INTERVIEWER: Exactly what was his rationale?

AUTHOR: A handout would have irreparably weakened my wage-earning muscle. My wrong-headed theory was that by going into teaching I could gain three free months in which to write.

INTERVIEWER: Now wait a minute. Didn't you just say you had not yet been to college?

AUTHOR: I did, but at that time the legal minimum for a grade school teacher in Alaska was a high school education.

INTERVIEWER: So your fellow inmates were right after all. You are part Eskimo.

AUTHOR: The place I went was the Aleutians, and the people who lived there were Aleuts, pronounced *alley-oots*.

On the Window Licks the Night

INTERVIEWER: And how did your writing go in your new teaching post?

Instead of answering, the author rises and goes to a closet where manuscripts have been stuffed like dirty clothes by a newlywed who hasn't yet learned the art of housekeeping. He tries to slip out a few, but breaking the jam brings dozens down onto the floor, and now I notice they all have one thing in common. Each has been so heavily overwritten it is almost illegible.

2

The island rose above the horizon, dark and bare as the fin of a shark. Its outline was already disappearing when scattered lights appeared which were hardly distinguishable from the evening star and others low in the sky. The lights were two-dimensional like those in the sky itself, giving no sense of distance, and all I hoped was the locals knew where we were. Ever since we'd left Cold Bay the crew had been drinking "sourdough," a white liquid like pancake batter, and the unhurried way they put the jug to their shoulders gave no hint of our imminent arrival. It wasn't until we touched something solid, causing pilings to sway outside the windows, that I saw how the lights had come from a bank of houses which now were marked by people hurrying to and fro like schools of startled fish.

"Yes, sir," said a man, as I made my way along

John Mitchell

a dock full of missing planks. We were like two ants who meet by chance, but he had definite information to convey and I had only the briefest glimpse of the other villagers as they swung down into the galley, using the bar at the top of the companionway, like apes. As we walked blindly into the night, I was trying to assess this place, and the sod spoke eloquently of recent rains, while breakers on the point were evidence of wind somewhere. I even sensed the school agent's greeting was not one of deference, rather the expression of a personal philosophy which forgave school teachers as well as drinkers. Showing me through a darkened doorway toward a heater's glow, he left me alone as I had been all the way from Cold Bay, sitting in the galley, in fact clear from Anchorage on Reeve Aleutian Airways, where I was the only passenger. Far from being displeased, I welcomed this freedom from being called to dinner just when the words were flowing, from whispered conversations meant to rouse my guilt for inconveniencing others, and especially from the anguish others' faces showed on reading what I'd written. Three thousand miles away was still not far enough.

On the Window Licks the Night

You can write anywhere there is air and light, even at the bottom of the sea, and the school quonset resembled a whale's belly, round and ribbed as it swam through a universe on a course beyond my parents' reach. Leaving my suitcase just where it lay in the middle of the schoolhouse floor, I undid the catches and got out pencil and paper. I had been planning this moment a long time. As the revelers moved the party to one of the nearby houses, causing the ground to shake like jello, I set myself to the task of creating my own universe. I didn't know these people, but I did the ones back home. In my childhood dreams there'd always been a girl, but under pressure from my parents I'd just never had time to settle on the proper character. Flipping through my high school yearbook, I now enjoyed the luxury of searching for the right candidate. The enrollment had been a thousand students, but a few had proved camera shy. Their names were listed in a white square after the pictures of their classmates, which still offered a number of girls to choose from. Many I knew too well already: traditional beauties, cheer leaders, the elected officials of student organizations. Each had acquired a certain reputation, and many had already passed from hand to hand among my friends in what was really a game of musical chairs, so that now I wondered what would eventually determine whom they married. Probably when the music stopped, I decided. The last one I'd gone with had been none too bright, and here in the undersea world of Wosnesenski School I decided brains would be a prime requisite.

Finally I made my selection, a wistful looking girl in a frilly blouse, whose chaste appearance matched the loneliness I was already feeling. Although there was something slightly protuberant about her lips, suggesting the presence of braces, I felt this disadvantage was more than offset by the fact she was a member of the Honor Society, as well as of the Spanish Club, *Los Galdós*.

3

She paused at the top of the boarding ladder when my father fastened his eyes on her shoes. They were brown moccasins, each with a penny in the diamond-shaped window of leather that was sewn over the instep. Since she had fine ankles and unusually high arches, I was not surprised she found his glance disconcerting.

"Is anything wrong?" she asked, stepping back.

"Of course, not," I said. "Come on aboard."

"But I'm not sure. I've never been on a yacht before."

It was clear from her formally erect posture and the extreme effort she made to touch nothing, even to avoid falling, that she was telling the truth. As if to emphasize her naïveté, she wore a frilly blouse whose rough, uneven texture resembled that of a lily.

John Mitchell

"Let's go," I said, "tide and time wait for no man."

"Not until you tell me what it is."

My father turned away, leaving me to deal with a situation I knew too well already. It occurred every time I brought a different guest on the boat. Since the yacht had the bright, lustrous finish of a piano, no one was allowed to set foot on her in hard-soled shoes, and while my father's moccasins might look like my date's I knew their undersides were made of rubber slashed in waves, the trademark of the yachting fraternity.

"Why don't you try these," said my sister, emerging from the after stateroom with what looked like tennis shoes, but again would leave that fine, distinctive track, subtle as a thumb print.

By now my guest was beginning to sense a conspiracy, and I really couldn't blame her. "I'm sorry, but I only wear my own shoes."

"Have a heart," I said. "You'll spoil the weekend."

"That's your problem."

On the Window Licks the Night

For a while it looked as though none of us would be going to Catalina Island. Then my mother rose out of the galley like an Egyptian queen from a tomb, her hair piled on top of her head. She was carrying a tray of drinks, each glass bearing the ship's name sandblasted below the lip, *Fat Cat*. While the names of pleasure craft tend to be eccentric, it was only because it was bad luck to change a boat's name that my parents had kept it.

"Won't you have something to drink, Freya, a beverage or a juice?"

"Thank you."

I was glad to see my date step back on the yacht, seating herself carefully in the cockpit and straightening her slacks as if preparing for tea. For a while everything appeared to be all right. We dropped our mooring line, which ran between two buoys, fore and aft, and started motoring out between the arms of San Pedro's inner breakwater. Once in the outer harbor we would be able to raise the sails, which would free us from the nauseating odor of our own exhaust. Unfortunately the moment of relief and silence arrived too late, for long before, Freya began showing signs of seasickness even though there was no swell.

"Feed her soda crackers," said my father, who was clutching the helm with one hand and his drink with the other. He wore a billed cap and his nose was covered with zinc oxide, but the voice of authority was unmistakable. My mother and sister, meanwhile, had begun playing cards, ignoring Freya completely in what I knew was a conscious effort to remind her she hadn't changed her shoes. This time she followed orders perfectly, but couldn't seem to get beyond her crime. Much to my embarrassment, she would swallow a cracker, throw it up, then try to chase it with a sip of water. However modest she might have been about her feet, there was no way she could hide the contents of her stomach. At first I could detect traces of bile in her vomit, but soon all that came up was clear liquid slightly warmed and laced with saliva. Meanwhile that white shirt I'd admired so much had turned into a hospital shift as she slowly sank to the cockpit floor.

It was a relief for all of us to reach Howland's

On the Window Licks the Night

Landing on Catalina Island, where another pair of buoys waited with a line strung between, this time heavy with moss since it was lifted onto deck only on weekends.

"Why don't you let South take you for a row in the dinghy," said my mother, who was growing bored with what she interpreted as Freya's answer to her game of cards.

"I'd rather go ashore," said Freya, still gulping like a dog having a nightmare.

"I'm sorry," said my father, "but it's private property and they don't allow boaters on the island."

"The danger of fire," my sister added, ever the claque.

"Come on," I said, hoping against hope my date would straighten up, "the dinghy will help. Every boat has its own sea."

"It doesn't appear that I have much choice, does it?" Freya looked at the three of us before starting down into the cabin to change.

In a short while she reappeared in a two-piece bathing suit, and although her face was paler than the shirt she left below, strong legs denied her recent appearance of physical weakness. There was also something feminine in her hips which hair styles and cosmetics could not duplicate, which was how my mother, and to a lesser extent my sister, established their sex.

"Won't it tip over?" said Freya, speaking directly to me as she entered the punt which was bobbing beside the yacht.

"Just grab both sides," ordered my father, who was standing at the rail, looking down. "That way it can't turn over."

"He's right," I said, when she didn't respond.

"Bon voyage," said my mother, as we started across the bay, and I for one was glad to be away from the influence of my family. I was watching Freya, whose elbows were slightly reversed as she leaned back, graceful as a mermaid on the rear thwart. It was the moment our eyes should have met, establishing an understanding, but I could see she was still not ready for that.

"Do you dive?" I said, tossing out the little Danforth when we came to a spot where you could still

On the Window Licks the Night

reach abalones without scuba gear. She didn't answer, concentrating instead on holding the anchor line as I rowed back on it. The dinghy's anchor was a carbon copy of the one on the yacht, only smaller, as was the dinghy itself in trim, color, hardware. As were the people in this bay each mirror images of the other: the men with drinks in their hands and visions of vomit on their caps, the women like black widow spiders from whom you didn't escape easily—all except her. She was different.

"What are those rusty screwdrivers for?" she said, as the rock wall of a grotto loomed above us. We had reached the area of the beds.

"They're to lift off the abs. You've got to get under them quickly or they start sucking, and then the only way you can get them off is to break their shells."

"What do you do once you get them off?"

"You can either bring them back to the dinghy, or if you want you can stockpile them inside your trunks like I do. They stick to your stomach and you don't have to make so many trips."

"Won't they hurt you?"

John Mitchell

"They feel funny, but no."

At last our eyes met, and I could see she had only been waiting to see if, like my father, I was in love with the sound of my own voice. "All right, I'm ready."

4

The next day I looked out to see where this venture had landed me, half expecting to face the colorful house flags of the yachting crowd at Catalina Island. Instead, I had trouble believing I was still in the United States. The village of Wosnesenski was located on a windy strand which opened onto a horizon so blank I could actually see the curve of the earth. Its unpainted dwellings had the bleached, unhurried look of tombstones, and around them nothing stood but the skeletons of last year's Christmas trees which had come compliments of the Alaska Steamship Company. In a vain attempt to sustain the season's cheer the people had used them to landscape their houses, but without roots the scrawny trunks looked more like a castaway's calendar of years marooned.

Even more oppressive than the absence of trees

John Mitchell

was the almost total lack of color, and it was for this reason I welcomed the American flag, which hung over the blackboard, and immediately opened the new books which were waiting in packing cases in the corner. They were color-coded: green for sixth, yellow for second, orange for third, and so forth. For every text there was a workbook to match. On thumbing through a few, I saw they were not particularly good books, at least when compared to the older volumes on plank shelves along the walls—*Aesop's Fables, Pilgrim's Progress, Robinson Crusoe*—but I also realized the generic stuff would have one signal advantage for me. After using the blackboard to post the assignment for all eight grades, I could retire into the teacher's quarters at the back and get on with my writing.

"Good morning, teacher," said a child, who was bolder than the rest. For some time I'd been aware of advancing shapes. First they took cover behind the nearby houses, then under the dead Christmas trees, and finally in the hollows of the land itself, which this morning smelled of rain and vomit.

"Come in," I said, "and take the seat that fits

On the Window Licks the Night

you best. The assignment is written on the board. If you have any questions, I'll be in the teacher's quarters."

At this point it seemed I needed only to go on writing to escape my parents' influence entirely. The girl of my dreams was already taking form.

5

The auditorium was a raised peacock fan of note-taking students whose symmetrical pattern derived from their rigid adherence to the latest styles. Each was committed to the protective coloration of the undergraduate experience, and not even the tumbling books occasioned by my fall could shake their collective poise. It was then I saw her, distorted as if by my own preconception, and at first I thought I'd made a mistake. To begin with, her face was shorter than it had been in the yearbook and she was wearing glasses. Instead of gazing wistfully at the lecturer, she was helping him through a clumsy discussion of *E. coli* with her lips. I recognized the collar of the frilly blouse but not the lavender angora sweater over it. Generally, she had the look of a childhood friend you know hasn't changed but now

John Mitchell

must be approached through a maze of social mannerisms.

"Is this place taken?" I said, dropping into an empty seat beside her.

Without taking her eyes from the lecturer, she offered me her copy of a mimeographed sheet which had been going the rounds, and after glancing over it I was reduced to reading the advertisement on her pencil, which I suddenly realized came from our home town.

"Fosselman's," I said. "You know it's been a long time since I had a milkshake there. You remember, they were so thick you couldn't suck them through a straw, and if you tried to drink them they would gang up on you and spill all over the table like a bottle full of catsup."

For the first time our eyes met, and once more I was shaken by their difference in appearance. Instead of being filled with youthful innocence, as those in the yearbook had, the glitter of her lenses made them look almost cynical.

"How is it you know about Fosselman's?" she inquired.

On the Window Licks the Night

"I should know the place. I live less than a mile from there."

"But I don't see how you could. I mean I know all the people from our school who went to *The Farm*, and you're not one of them."

"I'm not a student here, I'm just visiting."

"Do you mind if I ask who?"

"You."

By now our whispered conversation was causing heads to turn, all except the lecturer, who plowed right on:

"*E. coli* is a real stinker. He will enter your intestinal tract and take control of the amoebas there. Reprogramed, as if by some mad computer genius, they will then turn on the host and injure him or her."

"Are you following any of this?" I asked.

"I was until a few minutes ago."

"Come on, let's get out of here. I feel like I'm getting the trots."

She didn't move. "I'm sorry, but I'm not dating this quarter."

John Mitchell

"How come, have you joined the Movement or something?"

"I'm not political. It's a question of trying to do justice to my parents' sacrifice."

Except for the noise of our voices the lecture hall had grown absolutely still, and I thought now was the time for a dramatic exit. Making my way between the backs of chairs and the knees of semi-cooperative students, I was not surprised to hear the echo of footsteps behind me. I had created a situation which I must now make good or lose the purpose of my visit. I was not so much bent on a conquest as creating a whole new world.

"With a fellow townsman you wouldn't have to dress," I said, the moment we were out the door. "Isn't dressing what takes all a girl's time?"

She took off her glasses and the eyes looked tired. "I think I remember you now. You're the wolf who used to show up every morning at school in a classic phaeton with a different girl. One time you even drove it up the auditorium steps."

"That's not quite accurate. Some of my friends carried it up there and I had to drive it down."

On the Window Licks the Night

"I think it's time to say goodbye."

"To this sham, you mean!" The atmosphere of a dude ranch had never struck me so forceably. For as far as the eye could see, red rooftiles created a kind of magic farmland in the sky, and for a moment I was back in the family albums. *The Farm* had been my parents' alma mater.

"Come on, don't be so hard-nosed," I said. "Let's go over to Sticky's and have some ice cream."

"I'm afraid I don't know where you mean."

"Of course, I'd forgotten you've only been on *The Farm* a short while. It's what they used to call the local Fosselman's."

She looked at me a moment longer, and I could see she was making her decision. "I'm really not hungry."

"Freya!"

I watched as she turned and started back into the auditorium, which was down the way from the Neo-Byzantine church which had lost its dome in the earthquake of 1906, better known for the great San Francisco fire. Behind it lay the president's house, like an overgrown mausoleum, and beyond that the Coast Range, toward which students directed their songs and maybe even their prayers that the San Andreas Fault wouldn't slip while they were there.

"Hey! I've got news from the homefront. Your uncle just got promoted."

Freya ground to a halt, her back still toward me.

"They made him head of Cal Tech's Jet Propulsion Laboratory."

She spun on her heel. "What are you, some kind of weirdo?"

"No, someone who loves you."

The tramp of feet disguised her cry, which I could tell from the expression on her face was not so much one of rejection as of sheer helplessness and frustration.

"You don't even know me," she yelled. "I doubt very seriously if I'm the person you think I am."

"But you are."

I could see she sensed the doubt in my voice, and I wanted to tell her it had nothing to do with her. It came from the undergraduates who even now were marching past us, looking like farmhands in

On the Window Licks the Night

their washed-out jeans. I had expected to see cadres of fraternity men wearing corduroy trousers as a sign of rank and addressing each other as, "Hi, gents," as they had in my father's day. Instead, what caught my eye was a biker tearing after a fellow on a motor scooter, shouting, "You fucking hamburger!"

6

A heavy-set man with an honest face and the appearance of what my own mother would have called "good horse sense" opens the author's door and looks in, introducing himself as the patients' rights advocate. It was he who first telephoned me about doing the interview, and I haven't forgotten his caveat. "You can always tell when they're going to hit you. You can see it in their eyes."

"Is everything all right?" he says.

"Fine," I say, "it couldn't be better."

The door closes and I wait for the lock to turn, but this time the bolt is silent.

INTERVIEWER: I'm sorry, but I'm completely lost.

AUTHOR: Why is that? When you took the off-

John Mitchell

ramp on *Interstate 101*, did the print on the street signs suddenly get too small for you?

INTERVIEWER: There's nothing wrong with my eyes. My problem is I don't know whether we're supposed to be in California or in Alaska. Are you really seeing this girl or not?

AUTHOR: Yes.

INTERVIEWER: Which?

AUTHOR: Do you know Jack London's *The Star Rover*? The hero, Darrell Standing, had the power of metempsychosis, or what we call the transmigration of the soul. Far from confining himself to California and Alaska, he traveled throughout history, reliving past lives.

INTERVIEWER: So you didn't return to California.

AUTHOR: I went there every day between classroom assignments.

INTERVIEWER: I'm surprised the parents didn't object to this practice and report you to the Department of Education.

AUTHOR: Under ordinary circumstances they might have, but the residents had had a bad expe-

On the Window Licks the Night

rience with the previous teacher, a recent widow who had called too many PTA meetings and tried to bribe the children to tell her what went on at parties. The result was I rarely heard an adult voice, and the children could be kept quiet by utilizing those colorful workbooks, or if necessary the oil drums in the yard, which made cold sitting.

INTERVIEWER: Even though you were beyond the arm of the law, you felt no responsibility for those poor benighted souls?

AUTHOR: On my arrival, the most striking feature of the school was the wall over the folding couch in the teacher's quarters. It was covered with pin-ups of Little Bopeep and other nursery rhyme characters. They were the last thing I saw every night before I went to sleep, and they never failed to remind me of the immortal messages prisoners leave on the walls of their cells, sometimes in their own blood. While the former teacher's was one of unmitigated suffering, mine would be the wonders of a drugless trip.

INTERVIEWER: Would it be accurate to say that all writing is a form of pathological escape, then?

John Mitchell

AUTHOR: Good writing, yes. Bad writing takes place when that deep, inner sense of dislocation goes away. That was what happened later, but what I did here was still legitimate. How potentially fertile I was can be seen in the fact that in the very next story I brought Freya to Alaska to keep her out of my parents' grip.

7

The little radio had importance for us only because it was the first thing we ever owned. Each of us had been living with radios all his life, but like most young couples we thought everything we did was new. The radio was practically hollow. Lacking the usual AC components, the maroon plastic case masqueraded as a substantial table set, when in reality most of the space inside was devoted to a heavy duty battery. After we got back from the Aleutians, I wanted something I could just plug into the wall and turned this symbol of our love over to Freya's uncle, who was an electronics engineer and said he could easily convert it to AC. Like so many of our other first possessions, the property was passed on to younger members of the family, but by then it didn't matter anyway. The radio had betrayed us.

There are two indelible memories which remain

John Mitchell

from that period. I am standing over a spring which bubbles up from under an outhouse. The health authorities have tested the water and claim it is free of coliform bacteria. I am wearing the blue yachting sweater my mother knit me in better days, ski pants with tapering legs which my father gave me, also in better days, and a pair of logging boots I bought myself. The boots are so new the shiny black leather makes them appear almost orthopedic, and on their raised heels I totter drunkenly as I lean down to scoop out the sulfurous liquid. I am drunk with power.

The same aura of grandeur transfigures the school, where Freya and I sleep on a couch which turns into a bed if you pull the back forward until it clicks, then let it fall. If so tamed, it offers the choice of the soft, saggy seat or the back itself, which is round and hard as a crowned highway. As the gentleman, I take the raised surface because I really don't care. I have never been so high.

The next day each of us was a little sobered. Instead of king and queen of Wosnesenski, we were

On the Window Licks the Night

teacher this and teacher that. Afraid the children would sense my hubris, I could only insist they call us by my family name, preceded by the conventional Mr. or Mrs., which they absolutely refused to do. Instead, they would use our given names behind our backs, which to me was an infernal piece of cheek, given the high nature of our presence here. It made no difference that within the community itself young and old alike went on a first-name basis, and I was about to make an issue of it with the school agent when Freya pointed out that all of these people carried Russian blood and so were products of a culture in which first names were a perfectly acceptable part of formal address: Cyril Vladimirovich for Count Bezukhov, Marya Fëderovna for Empress of Russia. Since I was reading Tolstoy's *War and Peace* between classroom assignments, I should have known.

As soon as we accepted the students' "respectful" familiarity, the strain between us eased. Unlike their stateside counterparts, the children on Wosnesenski Island loved school. The occasional packages from missionary agencies and even the vapid, but garishly

John Mitchell

colored, books were the only entertainment in thousands of miles. One little boy ate a tube of toothpaste before we could stop him.

Meanwhile the radio sat quietly on the formica table in the teacher's quarters, keeping company with the bottles of vitamins which Freya's mother sent to keep us from getting beriberi. Not only was there no place to plug the radio into the wall, but even the big battery brought in no signal. Much to our disappointment, all radio communication in the Aleutians was done by short wave.

But of course we didn't know that in the beginning, and one day I had a bright idea. To restore a tiny part of our former lives I would set up an external antenna. With that, I was sure we could at least reach Kodiak, which was only five hundred miles away. To make things easier, there was wire in abundance. During the Korean Conflict there had been a military installation on the island, and the abandoned barracks under Big Mountain were festooned with the stuff. It was as though a jungle had once grown beside Drunken Harry's Lake and then, owing to some inexplicable climatic change, died,

On the Window Licks the Night

leaving all the vines and creepers shrunk to copper wire. The minute I clicked on our magic instrument I was hearing voices, not Kodiak, but the islanders themselves. Freya's uncle later explained it as a harmonic.

We were eavesdropping, which of course is the least bit dangerous, and right away these people without mouths or ears were heard to speak. Although you might not like a voiceless culture, you could accept it if that was what it was, but it wasn't. With the help of ships' radios, some of which had been moved into homes for the winter—they kept only enough boats commissioned for emergency purposes—our little kingdom of thirty-two souls suddenly turned into hundreds, ranging all the way from Perryville in the east to Isanotski to the west, including places such as Ikatan, Sanak, Belkofski, and Unga in between. As CB buffs have since discovered, radio talk is a language all its own: witty, ribald, familiar, pontifical. Not only that, but on Wosnesenski Island its faceless practicioners forced me to revise my whole theory about them. They were far better read than I'd thought, far sounder in their grasp of world affairs, so that I had to hurry *War and Peace* just to catch up to the point where they were now. The bad thing was that they still failed to recognize our pre-eminence as the man and woman on the wedding cake.

It was almost to be expected that the children should grow bored with us, but I wouldn't have known the immediate cause had I not been eavesdropping on a set which even their parents would never have suspected could reproduce their voices. Wosnesenski Island was about to play host to one of its favorite daughters, Natalia, and her new husband, Sonny Boy. They were due to arrive that very morning on their fishing boat from King Cove. I gathered that as late as last year Natalia had been the arms-around-the-shoulder favorite that Freya was now. It was always interesting to see my wife and the kids go off at recess down the old military road. Not only did her comparatively short stature make her indistinguishable from the students, but she was in reality almost the same age. During the time troops had been on Wosnesenski, school had been closed, so that now most children were four or

On the Window Licks the Night

five years retarded. When the squawk of the radio explained why this morning the names whispered behind hands were those of Natalia and Sonny Boy, instead of Freya and South, the harshness of my exile knew no bounds.

About midmorning a horn sounded in the harbor, and the entire class rose as if dismissed for recess. I saw there would be no point in trying to stop them. I would have been defied, but even more hurtful the illusion I'd been nurturing would have been pushed like a pie in my face. It remained only to see what the devilish instrument was talking about.

Following the class at a discreet distance down the rickety dock which none of the islanders would lift a finger to repair, I saw what I now recognized as a salmon seiner whose black puffs of smoke indicated the need for a complete engine overhaul. Then Freya's predecessor appeared, electrifying, as only a town permanent could make these local women. Not only was Natalia the fattest, most homely woman I had ever seen, but Sonny Boy was a movie star, a darker James Dean here in this windswept archipelago where not even talent scouts dared to tread. It was clear from the stalwart way he pushed her up the ladder and then carried their bags down the broken dock that all he knew was that he was a male and she was a female and that he was probably lucky to be a hen-pecked husband here at the ends of the earth, or if not the ends, "at least you could see them from here," as the saying went. Were it not for the radio, they probably never would have met. It was already becoming obvious through the children's elated screams that Natalia had come to town to show her former people the cat we'd been hearing about for days on the radio. Her complaint was Sonny Boy had cut off its tail with his pocketknife. His story was the tail had been caught in a door slammed by the gale.

Freya was aghast. "What is it?"

Although my wife was disguised in an old woolen coat which was now held together with safety pins for buttons, and had taken to wearing a bandanna like the rest of the island women to protect her ears against the cold, we still knew that under that ugly cover her beauty lived, whereas Natalia had never known the word.

On the Window Licks the Night

"Well, try to look at it this way," I said. "I got you out of a yearbook, and you ran away from home because your mother made you take too many vitamin pills. Everything depends on force of imagination. It's just your idea against someone else's."

8

INTERVIEWER: So much for trying to establish a school of the north. It sounds as though you were near the edge.

AUTHOR: Not yet, although I will say that in a nearby bay I had recently mistaken a bald eagle for the Virgin Mary.

INTERVIEWER: Sounds like hallucinating to me.

AUTHOR: No, when seated its unusual size, coupled with its white head and folded wings, would have fooled anybody. It was not until I returned to California that things began to unravel seriously. Following my departure for Alaska, my father had been made chairman of the school board, and one of his first acts was to iron-ball my high school. Somewhere he'd learned that the main building was not properly pinned to its foundations, which provided him with the excuse he needed to dissolve the

John Mitchell

union between Freya's community and ours. She, of course, had no idea I was even thinking of her, much less putting it down on paper. Still, I found something premonitory in the way he said her neighborhood wasn't paying its fair share of taxes. His mania for self-reliance reached into all areas, and here his position was that my sister would get a better education in the new facility our wealthier district could afford. You can imagine how I felt on returning home with my modest parcel of stories under my arm, anxious to be recognized as a budding writer, and finding old friends would hardly speak to me.

INTERVIEWER: Your father had hurt you, but surely it was unintentional.

AUTHOR: That's easy for you to say. *Persona non grata* in my own community, I had only one thought and that was to find the real Freya. As I had foreseen, she had gone on to college, and after making a few discreet inquiries I was not surprised to find she was attending my parents' alma mater. Such was the power of the written word, which I was now certain would be my salvation. At first she wasn't keen on

On the Window Licks the Night

my intrusion into a life she'd worked for years to achieve, but the fact we were from the same high school made her trust me, and little by little her resistance weakened until finally we were only a few pages behind what I'd already achieved on paper.

INTERVIEWER: At least that part of your plan was working. How about your writing?

AUTHOR: Blocked. At first I attributed the lack of ideas to the influence of my parents, which seemed to follow me everywhere like smog, little realizing that in finding Freya I had largely solved my problem. Perhaps all adolescents experience a spurt of creativity when they encounter the adult world for the first time. What I do know is that without encouragement—what now seems like criminal encouragement—I might have settled down and done something sensible with my life.

INTERVIEWER: Was this when you entered a creative writing program?

AUTHOR: Not right away. At first I tried to go on projecting a separate existence in my mind, as I had in Alaska, but writing turned out to be the surest way to put myself to sleep. Sometimes we'd make love first and when I'd wake up Freya would be gone and I'd be lying in a sea of false starts and rumpled bedcovers. There'd be days when my only company was a neighbor raking his yard. First I'd hear the sound of the rake and then would come the odor of wet, smoldering leaves. Have you ever lived near a compulsive weed burner? Continual malaise. At first the university was tolerable only because it all took place outside the blinds, like movements on a stage.

INTERVIEWER: I'm surprised you would risk attending your parents' alma mater. Wasn't it precisely the life you wanted to avoid?

AUTHOR: What I'm trying to say is I needed the stimulation. On the day I knew I'd never write another word, I simply followed Freya to school. From there it was only a step to *The Farm*'s creative writing center, which was one of the nation's best.

INTERVIEWER: You make it sound rather easy. Normally they won't admit an auditor to a workshop class.

AUTHOR: You're forgetting the cunning that got me a job in the Aleutians, which I have often thought came from my maternal grandfather, the speculator.

On the Window Licks the Night

I crept up on the department, beginning in the creative writing library, where I found an original manuscript by John Steinbeck. It wasn't so good, and that gave me confidence. It wasn't until I'd become a familiar face in the halls that I even considered risking a confrontation. I was actually practicing knocking when I heard a human voice and, opening the door, saw Ms. Lure riding an exercise bike. When I cleared my throat to make her come down off her high horse, as it were, she told me rather tartly to go ahead and state my business, that she was listening. I told her I was a second generation legacy, and she admitted me without question to her class.

INTERVIEWER: One has to admire your commitment, but what ever could have possessed her?

AUTHOR: Later I found out that she was having trouble keeping up minimum enrollment.

INTERVIEWER: Was she any help at all?

AUTHOR: Ms. Lure did her best. She was available at all hours and always wrote legible comments. It was from her I learned the only useful thing I can remember from that period, which is that you must always tell the reader what he wants to know when

John Mitchell

he wants to know it. Where she fell down was as a writer in her own right.

INTERVIEWER: How did you learn that and what effect did it have on your work?

AUTHOR: During the meeting she'd referred to a story of hers in the annual *O. Henry* anthology, and after we were through talking I rushed back to the creative writing library and read it. It was disappointing, and so were most of the other prize-winning stories in the volume. It's surprising how a high school graduate can judge with accuracy, but I'd noticed on Wosnesenski that even children could tell the difference between the pap in their readers and Shakespeare, who when read aloud was well-received even by third graders. In the case of Ms. Lure's story, it was clear from the first sentence that her work was doomed to die with her, which was too bad because if you're having trouble writing it's very important to have someone else's work to feed on, which will at least give you the illusion of success. Since then, I've realized her pedestrian gifts are the rule rather than the exception in creative writing centers generally, which may be their chief fault.

On the Window Licks the Night

Once you admit a standard that is less than genius, success is within everyone's grasp, at least theoretically. Generally one forgets that, but fresh from the north I could still see the forest for the trees.

INTERVIEWER: I'd be interested in hearing what you did for Ms. Lure, if you still have anything that's readable.

9

I turned to face a neighborhood in which everything looked denatured: the street like a steamrollered sea, the houses expensive ice creams, the lawns upholstered poker tables. It was almost like returning to the age of innocence to see such things again, while at the same time I knew such effects were the result of workers striving tirelessly to convince a monied set of its own physical immortality. If your face fell, you had it lifted. If a tooth broke off, you had it capped. If your son was drafted, you called a general in Washington and got him off. I no longer had anything to do with such people, but given the situation in which we found ourselves I had no choice. The car had simply stopped.

Selecting a house whose trees were cut in the shape of boxes and cylinders, I started up the path. A lifetime member of the Garden Club, my mother

John Mitchell

had always had our oleander bushes sculpted and our line of cypresses carved, but it wasn't until I saw a similar residence that I realized how much like Shakespeare's at Stratford-on-Avon my home had been. Like so many in the suburbs, this house was of plaster supported by huge, hand-wrought beams which were now purely decorative. Surrounding the mullioned casements were rich vines meant to suggest England's rainy climate, yet the effect was that of an alpine ski helmet because of the trimming needed to make the windows open. The bricks in the walk had all been chemically aged before being laid.

Striking off down them, I knew how the tone would grow hollower as I approached the arched entrance, where I would be momentarily stopped by a heavy door which reproduced the curve of the arch in little. To approach our house had been like entering the wrong end of a telescope, yet arriving in a world of the up-to-the-moment. While the bell, set in a lozenge of hammered iron, recalled the strokes of the smithy who had made it, its clapper had been so tempered as to produce sounds of the greatest harmony, suggesting "Peace on earth, good will to

On the Window Licks the Night

men." The same contradiction was seen in the antique porch light, which went on and off with a timer.

After ringing once or twice, I knew instinctively the house was empty, which should have meant I turned and made my way back down the familiar walk the way I had come, which was how I'd been brought up and probably why I didn't. I had already noticed the place next door was one of those surreal monstrosities whose liberal architecture was belied by an electric release at the outer gate, which meant you had to sell yourself over an intercom system before you got in, which would have been impossible for me in my deteriorated state.

Taking my credit card from my wallet, I was pleased to feel it slide past the bolt. Unmechanical suburbanites, my parents had never had to take one of these things apart, which meant they were ignorant of the purpose of that tiny bolt which rides piggyback on the big one, and especially of the need to pull the door to until it clicks. All at once I was halfway to an upright phone with hanging horn, whose push buttons perpetuated the general sense of anachronism. It sat on a mahogany reception table of the sort it's hard to find anymore since everything today is made of pressed wood particles. I knew I was breaking and entering, but it would only be for a minute. All I needed to rid this neighborhood of my presence once and for all was to ring a service station and I would be a big hero to Freya, who was waiting patiently in our broken-down car.

Seizing the phone, I began to feel a little drunk, maybe on account of the odor of food cooking. My parents would never serve fish at home because the smell got in the air conditioning system and was spread about. It was funny how massive structures with thick drapes and shelves made heavy with unread books preserved such scents. The meal of the day had obviously been sauerkraut, whose rankness now came at me like an unwashed body. I knew there would be flowers on the grand piano, but didn't go near them for fear of leaving footprints in the deep pile of the carpet.

I might never have found out what those flowers were, except that after our car was towed away I realized that I had forgotten my wallet. It was of cashmere calf and had blended so perfectly with the

On the Window Licks the Night

hall table that I must have left without seeing it. Having searched every other place I could think of, including the garbage can at home and the garage where the car was towed, the English-style house in that upscale neighborhood was the only logical explanation. Knowing there might easily be some embarrassing questions and wanting to show Freya how much of a free spirit I used to be, I finally convinced her to come back with me "to protect me against myself."

I rang the bell perfunctorily just to show her how it sounded, and when nothing happened—as I knew it wouldn't—I was not hesitant about slipping my nail file behind the bolt, which caused the door to slide easily inward. She was impressed with my skills as a second story man, but for me the thrill of that was gone, and my interest lay much deeper in the interior, specifically in those flowers which had always desecrated the piano. Although we risked being caught in *flagrante delicto,* as my father would have said, I reasoned I had a better claim than ever to dispensing with the amenities, for these people had stolen my identity just as my parents had. As I strode across the oriental rug, I armed myself with the excuse that my family once owned this place and I had just come back to see it, maybe from a nuthouse. Fortunately, the need for Boy Scout preparedness was unnecessary. The rectangle of cashmere calf was right where I'd left it.

"Aha! They must have a big family."

"What makes you say that?" she said. I could actually feel her leaning against me.

"Because my wallet's here, my dear Watson. That means there were so many of them each thought it was the other's."

"How ingenious you are."

"Yes. They weren't careful like my parents."

Freya laughed. "I really think you should write detective stories."

"For now, the mysteries of the past are what interest me. What do you suppose they're cooking today?"

"It smells like some kind of beef, but I can't tell what."

"Let's go see."

"Don't you think we better get out of here, South?"

On the Window Licks the Night

"Wait, I've got to see if they've changed the flowers. Now watch your step." Without looking, I knew there would be a double step which led to the living room and whose only purpose was to increase its sense of grandeur. That vanity had once cost my paternal grandmother a broken toe which, because of her diabetic condition, had had to be amputated.

"Bermuda lilies. Now let's go!"

"You say you can't understand me. Well, this is your chance."

"But South, in jail we won't see much of each other."

While we were arguing, I managed to lure her out to the kitchen, where the food we were smelling turned out to be beef Stroganoff, and I even went so far as to change the flowers.

The upshot was, and using a different argument—this time that I needed to see the house for therapy—I convinced her to make repeated visits. To minimize the chances of being caught, I was careful to go back at the same time of day our car had stalled, but once inside I threw caution to the winds, laying my writing out in the spacious den with its unused fireplace and hidden jars of water meant to

John Mitchell

keep the mahogany paneling from cracking. I had days of unusual productivity, ideas coming right out of the woodwork, while Freya allowed herself to do the things an old-fashioned woman does: adjust the flame under the food, sort out the laundry, and empty waste baskets.

Eventually we came to think of this house as ours, which was why I was surprised one day, coming down the palatial stairs in my shirtsleeves, to see a stranger pushing in the door, her arms loaded with boxes. At first she didn't seem to see me, making me think I'd somehow grown invisible. Then, as though a time machine had broken, past and present came together with a jolt, and she began to shriek in that stagy way I knew so well.

"Don't be afraid," said Freya, rushing to the rescue, her voice full of a solicitude she usually saved for me. "We're not going to hurt you."

"That's right," I said, "you just got your schedule mixed up. We'll be out of here right away."

"Stay back!" The owner's cheeks were shaking like the leaves of the plants when I turned on the sprinklers, which I used to do to help the gardener,

On the Window Licks the Night

and I could think of nothing to say that would turn them off. Like my mother, she was obviously a person who lived near the edge.

Freya was definitely made of sterner stuff, having lived with me now for all of two months, and she stepped forward squarely to confront the owner, barring the telephone with her body. "You can call the police if you want, but first we have to take an inventory."

"An inventory?" said the woman, blinking as though a painful shaft of sunlight had suddenly pierced her tears. "I don't know what you mean."

"Yes, why an inventory?" I asked. There was something I didn't like about suddenly being shifted from the role of Sherlock to Watson.

"It's quite simple," said Freya. "I don't want her accusing us of being thieves, later."

"But I wouldn't take this stuff. I'm only here to prove I don't need it."

"I thought you wanted to show me a better life."

"Well, not exactly. To enjoy a place like this you have to work so hard your stomach is like a drum when you come home from work at night. My father

John Mitchell

used to collapse on the Louis XVI couch, and there was nothing we could do about it. My mother and sister and I would gather round to wait, and when he let a fart we all clapped."

"I think you're spoiled and selfish, and you'll never make a mystery story writer, or any other kind."

"You think I went clear to the Aleutians and ate seagull eggs just for kicks? You may not know it, but they lay three to a nest, and the way you collect them is to break one. Then if there isn't a bird in it, you keep the other two."

"Oh, why don't you just get out," said the lady, whose topiary hair-do was making her look more and more like a bad dream.

"You mean we can go?" I said.

"Yes, just go."

"Thank you." Whenever I filled my voice with unctious humility, I always got off. What I couldn't make Freya understand was how bad all this had been.

10

INTERVIEWER: Can we assume your relationship with Freya had hit some rough spots?

AUTHOR: Not only that, but Ms. Lure was saying that from her perspective my work had serious defects.

INTERVIEWER: I'm not sure I agree. I found some rather sharp observations on your childhood environment in that story.

AUTHOR: That's why for me it was a failure. My vision of Freya was collapsing.

INTERVIEWER: But not for technical reasons.

AUTHOR: Ms. Lure believed my basically sexist attitude was revealed when I made Freya willingly do the housework while I was writing.

INTERVIEWER: But wouldn't that be the normal response of a bored companion?

AUTHOR: Maybe, but it was uncanny how her

John Mitchell

seemingly unrelated prejudice illuminated trouble I was having.

INTERVIEWER: What about the earlier stories? You were certainly in love's springtime then.

AUTHOR: That's what shocked me most. She took exception to the expression "tide and time wait for no *man,*" instead of "no *one.*" Her feeling was the hero's relationship with the girl was doomed from the very beginning because he preferred a usage which has been in the language for over four hundred years.

INTERVIEWER: Who first set it down? Do you know?

AUTHOR: Credit is given to John Heywood in *Proverbs,* which appeared in 1546; but the phrase was repeated again by Robert Greene in *Disputations,* 1592; then by Robert Southwell in *St. Peter's Complaint,* 1595; and finally by no less a poet than Robert Burns in *Tam O'Shanter,* 1787. I've got lots of time.

INTERVIEWER: That's an impressive list of precedents, but I suppose you've got to allow for social progress. As Tennyson said, "The old order chan-

On the Window Licks the Night

geth, yielding place to new; and God fulfills himself in many ways, lest one good custom should corrupt the world."

AUTHOR: Isn't that exactly what the Russians said when they were brainwashing dissidents?

INTERVIEWER: It's too bad you were stuck with Ms. Lure, even though, as you say, she shed light on your failure to build an alternate universe.

AUTHOR: An odd attraction existed between us. I've thought about it a lot since I've been at Camarillo, and I believe we both represented something the other detested, at one remove. I have no idea what her early conditioning was, but for me her primary function was to keep me in touch with my parents. If you have an enemy, it's always better to know where he or she is, and she provided that touchstone. Since I was used to dealing with absolute rejection by my family, I felt comfortable in her presence because I always knew where we would end up. After one of her political lambastings, I'd retire to our cabin in Los Trancos Woods to lick my wounds, but I'd always be back for more. Not only did I need this negative stimulation to go on writing,

John Mitchell

but my instinct was still to use my imaginings as a point of departure in my relationship with Freya which, my doctors say, is quite the opposite of normal behavior.

INTERVIEWER: Is there anything else you want to read at this time?

AUTHOR: Nope, because even the irritation Ms. Lure produced in me wasn't enough to overcome my basic lack of aptitude for letters, and eventually I quit her class. It was for this reason I actually welcomed the news my father was planning a visit to *The Farm*. My sister was due to enroll in the fall, and he wanted to show her the campus where he had spent the "best years of his life." He even inquired into my finances, wondering if I could use a little help. Having borne the brunt of my ups and downs, Freya was not anxious for me to accept the invitation, saying his concern was just a come-on, and I admit I should have been suspicious when he declined to visit us in Los Trancos, suggesting I join him and my sister for a night up in San Francisco instead. Maybe the temptation of a free meal was just too much. At the time, a good dinner for Freya

On the Window Licks the Night

and me consisted of fried mushrooms on toast. After taking the commuter train, with its many starts and stops, to South San Francisco to meet the plane, I was so hungry I could have eaten a skunk asshole first. The road to dinner was equally long, beginning with a walk through the city—to build up an appetite, my father said—and ending at the Top of the Mark, whose nineteen stories we also had to climb. After the meal we went back to the St. Francis, where I was invited to read some of the work I'd been doing for Ms. Lure, and I actually welcomed the opportunity, although the result was much the same. According to my father, I should avoid heroes who were down-and-outers. His theory was that people had enough problems of their own without having to read about losers, and of course my sister agreed. What my father really wanted to know, and probably why he had avoided inviting Freya, was what my plans were for the future. I said they hadn't changed, and he wondered how in the world I was going to support a family, children being the natural result of "shacking up with a girl," as he so inelegantly put it. I told him I would simply practice ab-

John Mitchell

stinence, and his laughter almost brought the house police. The odd thing is the meeting got me writing again. I found I had regained the power to dream, although it was only a pale one.

11

Annabill was supposed to be a product of her parents' love, as witness the name, which combined the two of theirs. On a high-stepping campus like *The Farm*'s the compound sounded bucolic, but Freya remained a loyal friend because the girl had problems, chief among them her parents' divorce. Annabill had a reputation for being a man-eater, and I avoided her whenever possible, sometimes crawling along below the windows of the cabin when I saw her coming; but today I was in a temper and she caught me out by the pot-bellied stove, where I was burning books.

"Hello," she said.

"Howzit."

Without saying anything more, she swung first one leg and then the other over the picket fence that screened the service area, and I suddenly realized I was seeing her for the first time. She was tall, with chestnut hair so fine and shiny it looked artificial, tempting you to take those steps that were necessary to find out.

"She's not home," I said.

"You're such a funny person."

"It's been my experience that people grow funnier in direct proportion to the degree to which they feel themselves rejected. Around Freya I'm so ordinary it's boring."

"I don't believe it."

"I am!"

Calmly, Annabill stayed my hand, which was reaching forward to light the pot-bellied stove, which contained a number of classics I particularly objected to, and applied the match to a cigarette she was balancing.

"Let's go for a walk," she said, after getting it going.

"Have your parents gotten back together yet?"

"No, but I'm feeling better today. They've started a dialogue by tape recorder."

It must take one to know one, I thought, and

On the Window Licks the Night

finally I gave in. It was not often I let a stranger into my world, which now seemed tenable only when I was alone. You could not tell people that the potbellied stove stood like a windlass in a clearing of oaks which made the sky appear like the mouth of a well in which waves of heat shimmered like water. This was the true nature of the setting and needed no explanation, political or otherwise. On the other hand, I was more than aware that Annabill injected the very quality I objected to in "classical" novels. Would she or wouldn't she? Suspense.

"Just a minute, Annabill, I'll get my gun."

"Do you have to? I hate guns."

"I think it would be a good idea. The rattlesnakes are out."

She had to say that, I thought, as I went into the house. It was like the dialogue in those old novels, where everything had to act in opposition. Was there no other way to make life or a book interesting? One of the things I liked best about Freya was her frank attitude toward sex. With her it was never a game, but something too important and intense to be toyed with.

John Mitchell

"I hope you won't use that gun unless you have to," said Annabill, when I emerged with my Marlin .22. The lever action gave it the look of a much bigger weapon.

"The only reason you care about ecology," I said, "is because you've lost your faith in God, and it takes away your fear of death."

"There you go being insecure again."

We started into the trees, soon picking up a trail not visible from the clearing. Meanwhile I tried to recover the line of thought I'd been following before she came. I was attempting to figure out a way to write a book as honest as the air I breathed. Take the yellow jackets. They were always out looking for food, but I no longer feared them. When I was having lunch they used to drive me away from a jam sandwich, but lately I'd learned that a sharp blow did not allow them time to sting. Their small bodies made a cracking sound like eggs, which of course was not necessarily the kind of thing editors wanted. Judging by the long popularity of Victor Hugo's *The Hunchback of Notre Dame*, which was now stuffed in the incinerator, they cottoned to

On the Window Licks the Night

larger-than-life characters such as Quasimodo, the gypsy girl Esmeralda, and the sex-crazed priest Claude Frollo—gratuitous titillation such as I expected Annabill was likely to offer before we had gone very far.

"I don't like you pointing that gun at me," she said, even sooner than I expected. She had just tossed a burning cigarette into the dry California foothills, which I rather admired, but not her coquettishness.

"Don't worry. It's not loaded."

"You're always supposed to treat a gun as though it's loaded."

"You'll catch poison oak if you walk out there, Annabill." To avoid the .22, she was walking first on one side of the trail, then on the other.

"But I don't like your gun *looking* at me."

"Here, you take it."

Somewhat surprised, Annabill accepted the rifle, clasping it to her chest like a native gunbearer, and for a while we walked in perfect silence, which was how all art should be, I thought. In this way I could hear a twig crack underfoot even though it was buried deep in dust, while the blood beating in my ears made the steady, whispering sounds of a broom. Occasionally our steps would echo against an opposing hillside, creating the illusion of another party in the area, but usually it was so quiet not even the quail knew we were coming. It was for this reason I heard the rattler long before I could step on it, buzzing like one of those gourds full of seeds which musicians shake in Latin orchestras, except it lacked their jaunty syncopation.

"Why are you stopping?" said Annabill, who had begun to rock the rifle like a doll.

"A rattlesnake."

"Well, what are you waiting for?" She jammed the gun in my hands. "Shoot!"

"I thought you didn't like killing animals."

"A person doesn't always mean what she says." Insinuatingly, she thumbed back the hammer, showing more familiarity with a Marlin .22 than I would have thought she had.

"No," I said, delivering a few head-high kicks, which the snake easily avoided, going backwards like a train with controls at both ends. At the same

On the Window Licks the Night

time I saw how fiction ought to work. Image, not plot, should drive narrative. In this case what made the woods interesting was that they resembled an ornate gaming board and the snake the sinuous trail with larger squares at either end that parlor snakes conquer with a cup of dice. That was the truth and how you got from one end to the other was of little importance.

"Aren't you scared?" said Annabill, as the rattler disappeared into the underbrush, still keeping its head pointed toward us.

"No, not really."

"My whole life swam before me. I suddenly remembered what my parents used to call me."

"All right, what was it?"

At this point I felt her arms slip over my shoulders like one of those coats you wear without using the sleeves, but want to keep ready in case the weather changes. "They called me their little Petri dish."

12

INTERVIEWER: How did Annabill fit into your dream of Freya, if I may ask.

AUTHOR: You mean did I sleep with her?

INTERVIEWER: You said it, I didn't.

AUTHOR: I hate to disappoint you, although I found my evenings lonely. Like Ms. Lure, Annabill was a lesser dream I used whenever the idea of my girlfriend grew too insubstantial. Freya was completely wrapped up in her career, but I never would have stepped out on her for fear of diminishing myself. Beauty, as the poet says, is in the eye of the beholder.

INTERVIEWER: Couldn't you have gone on fantasizing her as you had on Wosnesenski? Surely she was no more distant now than then.

AUTHOR: That's what made it worse.

INTERVIEWER: I hope at least you'll admit she

never asked you into her life, which meant everything she did for you was just a favor.

AUTHOR: There's no doubt of it, but would it have been equally as useless for me to seek relief in someone like Annabill as it would have been to seduce Ms. Lure. Anyone who has ever been in love will understand. Whatever you do you're trapped, and I was doubly trapped because Freya stood wedged like a rotten stick in the jaws of my parents.

13

Our rental had a floor heater with a horizontal vent which attracted rats when you left it on pilot at night. They kept me awake with the noise of their claws, and at first I pretended I was still in Alaska by hunting them. Sometimes I used the .22, but that made holes in the walls and it was less risky to employ the landlady's Dandie Dinmont terrier, a mangy little animal but death on rodents. I'd go down into the basement with him under my arm, much as a miner takes a canary into a shaft, and he'd smell out the game. He was so small he couldn't do it alone, and I'd have to lift him from shelf to shelf, where he'd bark hotter and colder; but the moment he got a rat out in the open it was over in a second. One shake and its back was broken.

Some days I would wrap myself in bandages and go out into the woods. Although I was highly susceptible to poison oak, I had a theory that you had to touch it physically to experience a reaction, not merely contact airborne pollen, as I'd been taught. People would stop their cars and look at me as though I were a leper, but I knew what I was doing. I'd return to the cabin and remove my clothes as if they were radio-active, then take a shower. Next I'd sit out the incubation period, but I never got it.

There was always some way to keep busy. Under the front porch we had a nest of yellow jackets which would sting you just for looking at them. My first thought was to drown them with the garden hose. I thought by rushing forward with socks on my hands and jamming the nozzle down into the paper-lined hole before they were alarmed, I could wipe them out, but I was wrong. It's amazing how strong those bees are, walking right up against the stream, like robots. I can still see their wiry legs clutching the column of water, their feelers trying to sense the enemy, but here they were programed even worse than I was. There were so many of them I think they would have put me in the hospital if it hadn't been for the porch light, which I'd carelessly left burning.

On the Window Licks the Night

They attacked it mercilously like heat-seeking missiles and I was saved.

"Why don't you come to school with me?" said Freya, one day. "I don't know how you stand it here alone."

"I have plenty to do."

"But you're not even writing." There was a look in her eye that I'd come to see more frequently. It bordered on anger, but I preferred to think it came from the guilt she felt at not following the suggestions in the things I'd written. She behaved as though she had to go to school or else go crazy, when I believed it would have been just as easy to fulfill the vision to which I could no longer add, by staying home.

"All right, I'll drive in to *The Farm* with you. Then I can hitchhike back."

"You mean you won't stay."

"No, but it would be nice to have a fresh cup of coffee for a change."

Soon we were seated in a booth at Sticky's, along with a mix of other students who appeared like junior executives who have yet to receive offices of their

John Mitchell

own. Below the dark plywood panels a forest of legs and feet was in constant motion, and it was only by speaking loudly and listening carefully that you could manage to carry on a conversation. The hodgepodge of incomprehensible facial antics reminded me of a silent movie, and I didn't know why I had made the effort to come to this place. It was all part of a past I'd tried to outrun, but hadn't escaped.

"I say we should tip our hats and slowly ride away," I said, seized by more than my normal aversion to *The Farm*.

Freya was enjoying her coffee and now looked up in dismay. "It would be easier, South, if we were the only ones involved."

"We are the only ones involved, and even if we weren't it's our life." To make my point I casually raised my coffee cup to my head and tipped it. At Sticky's, to save dish washing, coffee was served in paper cones set in dark plastic holders which matched the paneling, and now I felt a warm trail of liquid running down my neck. As it came out of my sleeve like a wagon train from heavy cover, I was fascinated by the way it worked its way through the dry brambles of my forearm toward the uplands of my fist.

"But where would we go?"

"Alaska. I was always productive there."

"Aren't you forgetting the reason you had such freedom? The villagers were in reaction to the other teacher and except for that you wouldn't have had a paycheck."

"I was thinking of going into commercial fishing."

Freya rolled up her eyes. "And satisfy another deprivation of your early years?"

"I had you there once and you got along all right."

She looked at me coldly. "That was only in your mind."

"You're like Ms. Lure. You think my work is no good."

"I didn't say that. I love your work. It's just that fiction and life are often quite different."

"Which is the reason I want to get out." I put down the cup and began daubing with a paper nap-

John Mitchell

kin at the wet spot on my head, then down under my shirt. "I tell you the time has come to tip our hats and slowly ride away."

"I'll go anywhere but there."

"To act! To go!" I rose in the booth and replaced the cup on my head, which caused a momentary lull in conversation around us. At least some people understand how I feel, I thought. Although the cup and holder resembled a New Years bonnet more closely than they did a ten gallon hat, to me they could be anything you wanted. It was time to get back to first principles, and California was just not the place.

14

If the dream were not the Mayan temple of Chichén-Itzá, then what was it? I smelled vanilla and wintergreen, but what I saw were white towers against a green, treeless landscape. Maybe it was real, maybe it wasn't. Since I knew it was the sort of dream that would color the rest of my day, I decided to go out and look for it.

Even before I left our rental, I could smell the odor of rain in dry leaves. The droplets seemed to speak as they made their way from the topmost branches to the forest floor, near and far. The lighter foliage appeared bound up in gunny sacks as if for winter, which made it confusing, for around the structure in my mind nothing grew but native grass. This morning the air was so cold it felt like ice, but soon I was walking stripped to the waist, the arms of my shirt tied loosely around my hips. Now and

John Mitchell

then a breeze would blow through the woods and make me shiver, but my vision was like sleep, which walls out sound. I had my dream to keep me warm.

By the time I reached Portola Road, which was where we'd been parking the car to save gas, the dream had faded noticeably, but I was not about to be dissuaded. If the froth of the mind had any physical counterpart at all, now was the time to find out. I could go south toward La Honda or north toward *The Farm*, which seemed like the better choice since castles have to be built by somebody. Now the intuition was a mere memory, and in order not to miss anything I drove dead slow, pausing occasionally at likely driveways to see if my vision might be there.

One of the frustrating things about Portola Road was that it was screened on both sides by trees and barbed wire trellises of weeds, causing houses and fields behind to appear like objects seen through a fan. There were only half a dozen true openings in that many miles, and at the first of these I did see something white and majestic. It was a cloud which closely resembled Mt. Pavlov, which had lost a piece

On the Window Licks the Night

of its rim during its last eruption. The trouble was my dream had had no notch.

A short distance further on, by looking toward the Coast Range, I got a glimpse of the strange domes near Cold Bay, which had once been a military post, but whose importance now was chiefly as an airfield. It was a little hard to see in the rain-filled air, but judging from the domes' rusty, derelict appearance they were not the thing I sought. The same thing could be said of the old buildings, which could have been barns, but looked more like barracks blanketed with dust, the result of planes landing and taking off on the nearby airfield. There was nothing even remotely resembling my vision until I came to Lake Lagunita at the back of campus, and then a flash of light caught my eye. It was the Peter Pan Cannery at King Cove, where we had been forced to stop for fuel en route to Wosnesenski.

One of the reasons I so seldom visited the packing plant to which I sold my summer salmon was that it was very hard to reach. First you had to cross twenty miles of open water, some of it uncharted,

John Mitchell

and then anchor in an unprotected bay, which was always risky. If the anchor fouled, gusty winds could blow you out to sea, or worse, onto the beach. Although this sense of difficulty had not been part of the dream as I remembered it, it must have been there somewhere, for by the time the cannery stood white and glistening as the Taj Mahal, the odor had returned and so had the taste.

As I came into the lot behind the Neo-Byzantine church, I heard a low chorus of honks and was surprised to see geese standing stark as cooky cutouts on the lagoon flats. To see so many wild creatures all in one place was rare, even in a zoo, where it was usually a variety of species. At the same time my dream was taking on other new dimensions, for before my eyes a forest of masts was gradually disappearing, first moving sideways, then growing shorter as they descended toward the water. They were already launching boats!

A man appeared suddenly at my side. "Don't go in."

"But why?"

On the Window Licks the Night

"We're negotiating prices and need your cooperation."

"But there are a few things I have to get for the skiff." It was not that calking cotton and a pair of new oars were really important, but the shock that nothing like this had been prefigured in my dream upset me greatly. The goon at my elbow must have sensed my resistance, for his hand came heavily to rest on the door rearview.

"Look," he said, "it will only be a few days and then we'll all go fishing. Just be patient."

"You better be careful. My father built this place."

As I drove forward against his hand, the metal bent radically before overpowering his fingers. Then I saw a group of students on the office steps. These were company fishermen to whom the cannery always gave the best boats, and they looked angry.

"How are you doing, South?" one called out, as I moved toward them. Although he wore a jacket with white leather sleeves and a red vest of Turkish pile, I recognized him as someone who had once given me a tow when I was broken down, and now I didn't know what to do.

John Mitchell

"Fine." I couldn't even remember his name.

"Didn't someone stop you at the gate?" said another, not nearly so friendly, voice.

"Yes, but I saw they were launching boats." As he spoke, yet another mast looked like a tree that was being absorbed into the soil. The gardeners were really out in force this morning.

The one who sported the jacket of red and white wrinkled his nose as if the odor were bad. "I wouldn't know why."

"Some people have to learn the hard way," said another.

"If we stand up to the company this year," said a third, "next year we can walk in here with our hats on our heads."

At this point some locals I knew came out of the company office and passed very near us on their way down the boardwalk toward the newly commissioned boats. Some I recognized as members of the beach gang, but there were also fellows I'd never seen before outside a bar. Although these men were talking casually and cracking jokes about last winter's drunks, I also sensed a defensive posture in the

On the Window Licks the Night

way they moved, which wasn't surprising considering their motives. They were breaking strike.

"What will you guys do?" I asked the outsider who had once helped me.

"Fly home, I guess."

"But why don't you fish for Trident Seafoods?" Although he was Astoria based, I knew the man in the red and white jacket owned his own boat and therefore wasn't dependent on company equipment like the rest.

He looked apprehensively over his shoulder. "They might kill me."

A chorus of humorless laughter greeted his reply, and now I didn't know whether the onlookers were trying to scare me or were simply victims of their own delirium. I could see they were waiting for my answer, but with the odor of vanilla and wintergreen still strong in the air I decided the best thing for me to do was go back to Los Trancos and get a good night's sleep on it.

15

Dear South,

Freya's letter takes my breath away. I hadn't realized things had gotten so bad for you. Were it not for the fact your mother had a similar experience years ago, I wouldn't have believed it could have happened to anyone in our family, where the blood has been good for hundreds of years. You were probably too young to remember, but shortly after we bought *Fat Cat* she spent a three-month period in a sanitarium. There was no warning whatsoever. One day I came home from work and she didn't seem to know me, or you, or your sister. According to the maid, you had been teasing your sister all day long and wouldn't let up. I don't say this to distress you now, but to point out what seems to be a shared susceptibility.

As you can imagine, I've been cudgeling my

John Mitchell

brains relentlessly, and I think I've finally found a clue. At the time of your mother's breakdown she was rehearsing a play, and I know you do a lot of writing. Quite apart from religion, I'm not a praying man because I find wishful thinking very tiring. Frankly I'd rather work. There must be something about projecting the mind into the unknown that draws down a fellow's batteries, except when he's asleep. Then it's okay.

One of the reasons for my concern is that your mother and I are planning to sail *Fat Cat* around the world. With both of you kids gone, it's going to be a little lonely around the house, and it will be good for her, as well as for me. One of the stops on our trip will be Cold Bay, which I believe is near your old teaching post at Wosnesenski Island. I'm looking forward to seeing that country, which I know you found so very stimulating.

Please take the money I enclose and use it to improve your health. Your mother got well and so can you. I know how stubborn you are, but there are situations where we must look outside for help, and I believe this is one of them. I must say now

On the Window Licks the Night

how much I regret not seeing Freya while we were in San Francisco. It's not every girl who can write such a letter to a man who gave her something less than red carpet treatment, but I fear you may lose her unless you change your ways. In addition to reporting details which I find too painful to repeat, she tells me you have not been eating well, so for God's sake go out and buy some steak and potatoes. Hopefully by the time we get back, it will all seem like a bad dream and we can laugh about it.

Take care,
Dad

16

First test locks and inspect skylights to make sure no one has been on board in your absence. Examine gauges on all fire extinguishers to verify they are in good working order. Set life rings in their holders out on deck. Before turning on ship's power, look into bilges with a flashlight to ensure there is no sign of floating fuel. Check engine's vital fluids, including cylinder oil, marine gear oil, hydraulics, battery acid, coolant. Most important is to activate the engine room fan. This will expel any combustible gases which may have gone undetected. You may then risk pressing the starter button.

a
Prone the launching periscope
digging treetop tips to miller
gyroscopic interlude
invades the littoral of stark intent.

John Mitchell

                  b
Homeward fusion rotting stealthily
altogether running you make light
of dandelion flying include
under cover of ample morning.

                  c
Fairly cinder opening penultimate
the pot I'm nodding envelope
. . . .
. . . .

17

"I think I've lost you again."

"I finally got my wish," says the author. "My parents became illusions."

"So that is what you meant when you said you'd killed them. It was just a series of verses."

"It was the only thing I could think of to do to restore my image of Freya. Let's take a break."

"That's fine, but you'll have to tell me what a break is on this 'campus' of yours."

"Just sitting calmly, letting life come to me. I even take pleasure in the fact hair grows on my knees..."

"Hair on your knees?"

"Sure, look at yours. I'll bet they're completely bald where the fabric has been rubbing."

Together we go down the stairs of the dormitory, which closely resembles paintings I've seen of the old

John Mitchell

California missions, including their contingent of human prisoners, or "clients," as they seem to call them here. Just now some are playing baseball with the proverbial little men in white coats and from the looks of it, winning. Everything is bright with sunlight, but all at once the author seems more tentative than I've seen him at any time during the interview. It's as though he still can't accept his failure to build an alternate reality. The story in his eyes is that someday, somehow, through force of imagination, Freya will return.

THE END

Kailua, Hawaii
January 19, 1994